Daughters
of Passion

Faber
Stories

Julia O'Faolain was born in London in 1932. Her novel *No Country for Young Men* was shortlisted for the Booker Prize. She was brought up in Cork and Dublin, educated in Paris and Rome and married an American historian in Florence. She lived for many years in the US, and now lives in London.

Julia O'Faolain

Daughters of Passion

**Faber
Stories**

ff

First published in this single edition in 2019
by Faber & Faber Limited
Bloomsbury House
74–77 Great Russell Street
London WC1B 3DA
First published in *Under the Rose* in 2016

Typeset by Faber & Faber Limited
Printed and bound by CPI Group (UK) Ltd, Croydon, CR0 4YY

A CIP record for this book
is available from the British Library

ISBN 978–0–571–35194–7

There was a story about her in the *Mail*. A phrase jumped off the page: '. . . the twisted logic of the terrorist mind . . .' Journalists! She'd have spat if she'd had the spittle; but her mouth was dry. 'Violence', someone had said, 'is the only way to gain a hearing for moderation.' That was reckoning without the press.

The argument broke open, porous as cheese. *Cheese* . . . She could smell the reek of it, pinching her nostrils.

Thoughts escaped her. This was the twelfth day of her hunger strike and energy was running low. Half a century ago, in Brixton Gaol, the Lord Mayor of Cork had died after a seventy-four-day fast. A record? Maybe. But how *much* of him could have survived those seventy-four days to die? A sane mind? The ability to choose? Surely not? Surely all that was left in the end would have been something like the twitch in a chicken-carcass, a set of reflexes primed like an abandoned robot's? Her own mind was bent on sabotaging her will. 'Eat,' her organism signalled slyly to itself in divers ways. It slurped and burped the message, registered it by itch, wind-pain, cold, hunger, sophistries. Sum ergo think. But thinking used up energy. Better just to dream: let images flicker the way they used to do years and years ago on the school cinema-screen. Then too it had been a case of energy running low. The generator went on the blink every time films were shown in the barn and that was often, for the hall was constantly being remodelled. The nuns were great builders.

'Come,' they coerced visitors, 'come see our improvements.'

Change thrilled them. The stone might have been part of themselves: a collective shell. Meanwhile, on film nights, rain drummed out the sound track and a draughty screen distorted the smile of Jennifer Jones playing Bernadette. The barn was cold but discomfort was welcomed in the convent. Waiting for the centrally-heated hall put in time while waiting for heaven.

She missed the community feeling.

Her vision shifted. Bricks and mortar from the

nuns' hall had turned to butcher's meat. She was choking. Her throat had dried, its sides seeming to clap together. She pictured it like an old boot, drying until the tongue inside it shrivelled. It itched. Food could drive any other consideration from her mind. Images decomposed and went edible, like those trick paintings in which whole landscapes turn out to be made up of fruit or sausages. She could smell sausages. Fat beaded on them. Charred skins burst and the stuffing pushed through slit bangers in a London pub. Three sausages and three half lagers, please. Harp or Heineken. Yes, draught. Could we have the sausages nice and crispy. Make that six. A dab of mustard. Jesus! Eat this in remembrance. Oh, and three rolls of French bread. Thanks. Christ-the-pelican slits his breast to feed the faithful. Dry stuff the communion wafer but question not the gift host in my mouth. Mustn't laugh. Hurts. Where's the water mug? Tea in this one. They'd left it on purpose. The screws were surely hoping she'd eat in a moment of inattention. It hadn't happened though. Relax. Water. What a

3

relief. Made one pee and the effort of getting up was painful but if she didn't drink her throat grew sandpapery. You wanted to vomit and there was nothing to vomit. A body could bring up its guts – could it?

Sitting up made her dizzy. She felt a pain around her heart. Lie back. Her mind though was clear as well water. At least she was too weak to get across the cell to that tray without catching herself. They'd left it there with the food she'd refused this morning or maybe yesterday. Not that she felt fussy. Easier now though that her body was subdued beyond tricking her.

Conviction hardened. It had come with habit. Maggy was here through chance.

'I'm sure I don't know,' the head screw had said, 'where you think this is going to get you. It's up to you, of course, to make your own decision.'

Cool, bored. Managing to convey her sense of all this as childish theatrics and a waste of everyone's time. She knew the system and the system didn't change just because some little Irish terrorist wouldn't eat her dinner. She was fair though, abid-

4

ing by the Home Secretary's guidelines. Nobody had kicked Maggy or put a bag over her head. This screw looked as though such things were outside her experience which perhaps they were. One lot of prison employees might be unaware of what the other lot were doing. A clever division of labour: those needing clear consciences for television interviews and the like could *have* clear consciences. The best myths had a dose of truth to them.

It might have been easier if they *had* knocked her about: given her more reason to resist.

Dizzy had said, 'The trouble with you, Maggy, is that you're an adapter. I suppose orphans are. They're survivors and survivors adapt.'

She meant that Maggy listened to the other side: a woeful error since it weakened resolve. Look at her now ready to believe in the decency of that screw. 'Sneering Brit,' Dizzy would decide right off. She never called the English anything but 'Brits'.

'Ah come on, Maggy. *Be* Irish for Pete's sake. What did the Brits ever do for you or yours? Listen, it's a class war. Don't you see?'

Dizzy was of Anglo-Irish Protestant stock and had gone native in a programmed way. Her vocabulary was revolutionary. Her upper-class voice had learned modulation at the Royal Academy of Dramatic Art. This made her enterprises sound feasible, as though they had already been realized, then turned back into fiction for celebrating in, say, the Hampstead Theatre Club or one of those fringe places on the Euston Road.

Rosheen's style was more demotic. She sang in pubs and in the shower of the flat which Maggy had shared with her and Dizzy.

Another marthyr for auld Oireland
Another murther for the Crown . . .

More exasperating than sheer noise was the spasm in Rosheen's voice. Maggy suspected she got more pleasure from these laments than she did from sex. The two had got connected in Rosheen's life. She had married an unemployed Derryman who took out his frustrations by beating her until Dizzy coerced her into walking out on him. Missing him, Rosheen flowed warm water down her soapy body every morning and belted out verses about tombs, gallowses and losses which would never be forgotten. Defeats, in her ballads, were greater than victory; girls walked endlessly on the sunny side of mountains with sad but pretty names and reflected on the uselessness of the return of spring. Maggy despised herself for the rage Rosheen aroused in her.

'Well, it's all due to history, isn't it?'

The three had watched the Northern Ireland Secretary on the box some weeks before Maggy's arrest. Talking of how a political solution would make the IRA irrelevant – *great* acumen, God bless him! – he had the mild smile of one obliged to shoulder responsibility and take the brickbats.

He got Rosheen's goat. 'He gets my goat,' she said. Maggy winced.

'He gets on my tits,' said Dizzy to show solidarity. But the effect was different since Dizzy could talk any way she felt inclined whereas poor Rosheen was stuck in one register.

Maggy, who had known Rosheen since they were six, had for her the irritable affection one has for relatives. Also envy. They had made their First Communion side by side dressed in veils and identical bridal gowns and Rosheen had made the better communion. Maggy, watching through falsely closed lids, had been stunned to see ecstasy on Rosheen's rather puddingy face. She had been hoping for ecstasy herself and it was only when she saw it come to Rosheen that she gave up and admitted to herself that Jesus had rejected her. It was a close equivalent to being jilted at the altar and in some ways she had never got over it.

'Your First Holy Communion', Mother Theresa had promised, 'will be the most thrilling event in your whole lives.'

'Really?'

'Oh,' the nun conceded, 'there will, I suppose, be other excitements.' It was clear that she could not conceive of them. She had been teaching communion classes for forty years. Photographs of groups dressed in white veils lined her classroom walls.

'Strength will flow into you,' she promised. 'I don't mean', she smiled at Rosheen who had made this mistake earlier, 'the sort of strength Batman has.'

The others gave Rosheen a charitable look. They were practising charity and she was its best recipient. Charity was for those to whom you could not bring yourself to accord esteem or friendship and in those days it had been hard to produce these for Rosheen, whose eyes were pink and from whose nostrils snot worms were always apt to crawl. You had to look away so as to give her a chance to sniff them back up. Even then you could sometimes see her, with the corner of your eye, using the back of her hand.

And then Rosheen had made the best communion.

It was not utterly unaccountable. The nuns had mentioned that the last shall be first. Their behaviour, however, made this seem unlikely. They preferred girls who knew how to use handkerchiefs, scored for the team and generally did them credit.

Maggy recalled quite clearly how, having finally got the wafer down her throat – to bite would have been sacrilegious, so this was slow – and still feeling no ecstasy, she had opened her eyes. All heads were bowed. The priest was wiping the chalice. Could he have made some mistake, she wondered, left out some vital bit of the ceremony so that the miracle had failed to happen? Maybe he would realize and make an announcement: 'Dearly beloved, it is my duty to inform you that transubstantiation has failed to take place. Due to an error, you have all received mere bread and may regard the ceremony up to now as a trial run. Please return to the altar . . .' These words became so real to Maggy that she nudged Rosheen who was kneeling beside her. 'Get up,' she whispered bossily. 'We're to go back . . .' She was arrested by Rosheen's face. It was alight. Colour from a stained-glass window had been carried to it by a sunbeam and blazed madly from her eyes, her nostrils and the lolling tip of her tongue. Rosheen smiled, rotated and then bowed her head. She looked like a drunk or a painted saint: ecstatic then? Could she be pretending? Maggy considered giving her a pinch but instead bowed her own head and concentrated on managing not to cry.

She was crying now. Hunger made you weepy. She'd been warned. It made you cold too, although she was wearing several jerseys and two pairs of leotards.

Rosheen had never been so right again. Probably she should never have left the convent. Someone had told Maggy that she had wanted to enter but the nuns wouldn't have her. Then she'd married Sean. That marriage had certainly not been made in heaven: it was a case of the lame leading the halt.

'A pair of babes in the wood,' was the opinion of Sean's mother, Mairéad.

Mairéad had come to London some months ago to see Sean and dropped round to Dizzy's flat. Maggy had been the only one in.

'Tell Rosheen I don't hold it against her that she left him.' Mairéad was a chain-smoking flagpole of a woman, stuck about with polyester garments so crackling new that they must surely have been bought for this trip. 'Half the trouble in the world', she drew on her cigarette then funnelled smoke from her nostrils with an energy which invited harnessing, 'comes', she said, 'from people asking too much of themselves.' She coughed. 'And of each other. Not that it's Sean's fault either. I'm not saying that. It's his nerves,' she told Maggy. 'They're shot to bits. What would you expect? When that wee boy was growing up he seen things happen to his family that shouldn't happen to an animal.' She let Maggy make tea and, drinking it, talked in a practised way about misfortune. 'She's at work then, is she? Well give her my best. I'm half glad I missed her. I only wanted her to know there were no hard feelings. Will you tell her that from me? No hard feelings,' she enunciated carefully as though used to dealing with drunks or children or maybe men with shot nerves. 'I'd have no right to ask her to nurse a man in Sean's condition. I know that. He's not normal any more than the rest of us.' She had a high laugh which escaped like a hiccup: 'Heheh! He was never strong. A seven-month baby. I never had the right food. Then the year he was sixteen it was nothing but them bustin' in and calling us fucking Fenian gets and threatening to blow our heads off. Every night nearly. That was the summer of 1971. They wrecked the house; stole things; ripped up the carpet. Four times they raided us before Sean left to come here. He's highly strung and his nerves couldn't stand it. He still has nightmares. Ulcers. Rosheen could tell you. Sure it has to come out some way. He gets violent. I know it.' Mairéad stubbed out a cigarette and drained her tea. 'Have you another drop? Thanks. I'll drink this up. Then I'd better be going. I've been going on too much. It could be worse. You don't have to tell me. Wasn't my sister's boy shot? Killed outright. He was barely fourteen and the army said they thought he was a sniper. I ask you how could anyone take a fourteen-year-old for a sniper? You're from the south? I suppose all this is strange to you? I'm supposed to be here to get away from it all. You look forward to doing that and then the funny thing is you can't. It's as well I missed Rosheen. No point upsetting her, is there? You'll remember what I said to say, won't you? Thanks for the tea.'

Maggy saw her out and watched her walk away, turning, as she put distance between them, into a typical Irish charwoman such as you saw walking in their domesticated multitudes around the streets of Camden.

Dizzy, who got home before Rosheen, said: 'Don't mention the visit to her.'

'Mightn't she be glad to get the message?'

'Really, Maggy!' Dizzy sounded like a head girl – had *been* head girl when they were at school together, in spite or perhaps because of being the only Protestant. 'You have no sense of people,' she scolded. 'Rosheen has no sense at all.'

Maggy began to laugh at this arrogance and Dizzy – which was the nice thing about her – joined in. 'Seriously though,' she drove home her point. 'Rosheen could easily go back to that ghastly Sean. Just *because* he's so ghastly. She has to be protected from herself! From that Irish death wish. Surely you can see that she's better off with me.'

'With us?'

'With me. Don't be obtuse.'

Dizzy had been bossing Maggy and Rosheen since the day they'd met her. They'd all been about twelve at the time. Maggy knew this because she remembered that she and Rosheen had been on their way back to the convent after winning medals for under thirteens at a Feis Ceol. Maggy's was for verse-speaking and Rosheen's for Irish dance. Suddenly Rosheen let out a screech.

'I've lost me medal. What'll I do? The nuns'll be raging. They all prayed for me to win it and now I haven't got it to show.'

'It's winning that matters,' Maggy tried to soothe her. 'The medal isn't valuable. Come on. We'll miss our bus.'

'I'm not moving from this spot till I make sure I've lost it.'

Rosheen began to frisk herself. They were standing on a traffic island in the middle of O'Connell Street and it wasn't long before her manœuvres began to attract attention. When she unbuttoned her vest to grope inside it, a tripper with an English accent shouted: 'Starting early, aren't you? What are you doing, love? Giving us a bit of a striptease?'

Maggy spat at him. It was an odd, barbaric gesture but, remembering, she could again feel the fury of the convent girl at the man's violation of dignity and knew her rage could not have been vented with less. Give her a knife and she'd have stuck it in him. The man must have seen insanity in her face for he wiped the spittle from his lapel and moved silently away. Rosheen, typically, had failed to notice the incident.

'I've lost it,' she decided, buttoning her blouse. 'I'm going to pray to Saint Anthony to get it back for me.' She knelt on the muddy pavement of the traffic island. 'Kneel down and pray with me,' she invited Maggy.

'Here?' Maggy's voice shot upwards. 'You shouldn't be let out, Rosheen O'Dowd! You should be tied up. People are *looking* at you!' Being looked at was agony to Maggy at that time. 'Rosheen,' she begged. 'Get up. You're destroying your gym-slip. Please, Rosheen. I bet', she invented desperately, 'it's against the law. We're obstructing traffic. *Rosheen!*

But all Rosheen had to say was: 'You're full of human respect. Shame on you.' And she began blessing herself with gestures designed for distant visibility. Like a swimmer signalling a lifeguard, she was trying for Saint Anthony's attention. He was known to be a popular and busy saint.

'I'm off.' Maggy, unable to bear another second of this, stepped off the traffic island in front of the advancing wheels of a double-decker bus which stopped with a shriek of brakes.

'Are you trying to make a murderer out of me?' The driver jumped out to shake her by the shoulders. 'That's an offence,' he yelled. 'I could have you summonsed. In court. What's your name and address?'

'Magdalen Mary Cashin, Convent of the Daughters of Passion.'

'What's that? A nursery rhyme?' The man was angry. Passengers were hanging out of the bus, staring. 'Tell me your real name,' the man roared, 'or . . .'

Maggy ducked from his grasp, ran and, miraculously missing the rest of the traffic, made it to the opposite footpath.

'What's chasing you?' A girl of about her own age was staring inquisitively at her. 'You're from the Passion Convent, aren't you? I know the uniform. I may be coming next term.'

'You?' Maggy was alert for mockery. 'You're a Protestant.'

'Not really. My parents are, vaguely, I suppose – but how did you know?'

Maggy shrugged. 'It's obvious.'

'How? I'd better find out, hadn't I?' the girl argued. 'If I'm coming to your school?'

'You wouldn't be let come like that.'

'Like what?'

'Look at your skirt.' Maggy spoke reluctantly. She was still unsure that she was not being laughed at. 'And you've no stockings on! Then there's your hair . . .' She gave up. The girl was hardly a girl at all. Protestants almost seemed to belong to another sex. Their skirts were as short as Highlanders' kilts and their legs marbled and blue from exposure. 'Don't you feel the cold?' she asked. Maybe Protestants didn't.

'No. I'm hardy. Do you wear vests and things? I despise vests and woolly knickers!'

The intimacy of this was offensive but Maggy's indignation had been so used up in the last ten minutes that her responses were unguarded.

'I do too but I'm made to wear them,' she said and felt suddenly bound to the person to whom she had made such a private admission.

'My name's Dizzy,' said Dizzy. 'Is that your friend over there? I think she's signalling.'

'She's odd.' Maggy disassociated herself from the embarrassing Rosheen, who was indeed waving and rising and replunging to her knees. 'Don't mind her,' she begged. 'It's best to pay her no attention.'

'She's praying, isn't she? That's marvellous.'

'What?'

'She doesn't give a damn. Catholicism interests me,' Dizzy confided. 'I think Catholics are more Irish, don't you?'

'More Irish than whom?'

'Us.'

'You?'

'We *are* Irish, you know,' Dizzy argued. 'My family has been here since the time of Elizabeth the First. They're mentioned in heaps of chronicles.'

That, to Maggy's mind, only showed how foreign they were. The chronicles would have been written by the invaders. But she didn't mention this. What interested her about Dizzy was not her likeness to herself but her difference. It was clear that she lacked the layers of doubt and caution which swaddled Maggy's brain as thickly as the unmentionable vests and bloomers did her body.

'I found it!' Rosheen had arrived, all pant and spittle. She waved the medal excitedly. 'Saint Anthony answered my prayer. I knew he would. Isn't he great?' Rosheen always spoke of saints as though they were as close to her as her dormitory mates. 'Do you know where I found it? You'll never believe me: in my shoe.'

'This is Rosheen O'Dowd,' said Maggy formally. 'I'm Magdalen Mary Cashin and you're . . .?' She was chary of the ridiculous name.

'Dizzy,' said Dizzy. 'Desdemona FitzDesmond actually, but it's a mouthful, isn't it? So, Dizzy.'

'We're orphans,' Maggy thought to say.

'What luck,' said Dizzy. 'Wait till you meet my sow of a mother. She leads poor Daddy a dreadful dance. Drink, lovers, debts,' she boasted. 'Family life isn't all roses, I can tell you.'

The orphans were interested and impressed.

'Here's your tea.' The screw had brought a fresh tray. 'You'd be well advised to have it. As well start as you plan to finish and, believe me, they all eat in the end! Chips this evening,' she said.

Maggy smelled and imagined the pith of their insides and the crisply gilded shells. An ideal potato chip, big as a blimp, filled her mind's sky. The door closed; a rattle of keys receded down the corridor. Heels thumped. Teeth in other cells would be sinking through crisp-soft chips. Tongues would be propelling the chewed stuff down throats. If the din of metal were to let up she would surely hear soft munching. Her own saliva tasted salty. Or was it sweat? Did they count the chips put in her tray? Wouldn't put it past them. Tell us is she weakening. Keep count. They'd never. Wouldn't they just? Besides, to eat even one would surely make her feel worse.

There was no political status in England. No political prisoners at all. So why insist on treatment you couldn't get? They had made this point laboriously to her, then given up trying to talk sense to someone who wouldn't listen. People had died recently from forced feeding so they were chary of starting that. They followed the Home Secretary's Guidelines and what happened next was no skin off their noses. The country had enough troubles without worrying about the bloody Irish. Always whining and drinking, or else refusing to eat and blaming the poor old UK for all their woes. They had their own country now but did that stop them? Not on your nelly, it didn't. They were still over here in their droves taking work when a lot of English people couldn't find it. Rowdy, noisy. Oh forget it.

When you saw all the black and brown faces, you almost came to like the Paddies if only they'd stop making a nuisance of themselves.

A man had come to see her, a small man with a glass eye whom she'd seen twice in Dizzy's flat. He was from the IRA. He winked his real eye while the glass one stared at her. He had claimed to be a relative, managing somehow to get visiting privileges. She must play along with his story, winked the eye. Was she demanding political status? Good.

'They'll deny it but we have to keep asking. It's the principle of the thing.'

There had been a confusion about him as though he didn't know whom to distrust most: her, himself, or the screws. His dead eye kept vigil and it occurred to her that one half of his face mistrusted the other.

Impossible to get comfortable. Her body felt as if enclosed in an orthopaedic cast. She had a sense of plaster oozing up her nose and felt tears on her cheeks but didn't know why she was crying, unless from frustration at the way she had boxed herself

23

in like a beetle in a matchbox. She was boxed in by her ballady story. It didn't fit her, was inaccurate but couldn't be adjusted, making its point with the simple speed of a traffic light or the informative symbol on a lavatory door. She was in a prison within a prison: the cast. Slogans were scrawled on it: graffiti. She was a public convenience promenading promises to blow, suck, bomb the Brits, logos, addresses of abortion clinics, racial taunts. 'Wipe out all Paddies and nignogs now!' shrieked one slogan cut deep into her plaster cast inside which she wasn't sure she was. Maybe she'd wiped herself out?

She had committed a murder. Performed an execution. Saved a man's life.

Depending on how you looked at it. Who had? Maggy the merciful murderess.

Her story was this: she had been an orphan, her mother probably a whore. Brought up by nuns, she had lost her faith, found another, fought for it and been imprisoned. This was inexact but serviceable. If they made a ballad about it, Rosheen

24

could sing it in a Camden pub.

When she was very small the nuns told Maggy that she had forty mothers: their forty selves. An aunt, visiting from Liverpool, was indignant.

'Frustrated old biddies!' These, she asserted, were mock mothers. 'You have your own,' she said. 'What are they trying to do? Kill her off? What do they know of the world?' she asked. 'Cheek.'

'What world?' Maggy wondered. She was maybe four.

'Now don't *you* be cheeky,' said the aunt.

On what must have been a later visit the aunt reported the mother to be dead. Maggy remembered eating an egg which must have been provided for consolation.

'I'll bet they'll say it's for the best,' raged the aunt and began painting her face in a small portable mirror. 'You didn't love her at all, did you?' she interrogated, moistening her eyelash brush with spit. 'I told her not to send you here. She'd have kept you by her if she could. Children', the aunt said, 'have no hearts.'

The aunt too must have died for she didn't come back – and indeed maybe 'aunt' and 'mother' were one and the same? Maggy, when she grew older, guessed herself to be illegitimate, as there had never been any mention of a father. And so it proved when eventually she came to London and applied for a birth certificate to Somerset House.

'You don't know your luck. No beastly heritage to shuck off!'

Dizzy had come to the nuns' school to spite her mother who favoured agnosticism, raw fruit, fresh air and idleness for girls.

'Not that it matters where she goes to school!' The mother was mollified by the smallness of the nuns' fee. 'Nobody of my blood ever worked,' she said. 'Dizzy will marry young.' She spoke without force for she was to die of diabetes when Dizzy was fourteen. After that Dizzy's father became very vague and did not protest when she became a Catholic. Thus fortified, she was allowed by the nuns to invite Maggy home for weekends.

They spent these talking about what they took

to be sex and dressing up in colonial gear which they found in the attic. Much of it was mildewed and so stiff that it seemed it must have been hewn rather than tailored. There were pith helmets and old-fashioned jodhpurs shaped like hearts. Dizzy's father had served in Africa, although she herself had been born after his return to Ireland when her mother was forty-four.

'I'm a child of the Change,' she relished the phrase. 'I'm not like them.'

Who she wanted to be like was the bulk of the local population, and, on Poppy Day, she hauled down the Union Jack which her father had raised. He was apologetic but this only annoyed her the more for she felt that he ought to have known his own mind. Dizzy was eager for order and when she became a Catholic fussed unfashionably about hats in church and fish on Fridays.

On leaving school, Maggy won a scholarship to an American university. Coming back, after eight years there, she met Dizzy again in London. This was a Dizzy who seemed to have lost much of her nerve for she blushed when Maggy asked: 'Did you know I was in love with you when we were in our teens?'

This was a requiem for someone no longer discernible in Dizzy, whom Maggy recalled as pale and volatile as the fizz on soda water. Dizzy had had fly-away hair worn in a halo as delicate as a dandelion clock. Her skin might have been blanched in the dusk of her secretive house. Agile and seeming boyish to Maggy who knew no boys, she swung up trees like a monkey so that one could see all the way up her skirt. She was Maggy's anti-self. Once, in a spirit of scientific inquiry, they showed each other their private parts. Later, Dizzy discovered this to be a sin or at least the occasion of one.

'You knew,' she accused. 'You should have told me.'

Maggy was disappointed to find freedom so fragile and each felt let down.

Now Dizzy's skin was opaque, thickish. She had lost her charm, but Maggy, although she might not have liked her if they'd just met for the first time, was responsive to memory. She felt linked by a bond she could not gauge to this woman who had first alerted her to the possibility of frankness. Dizzy had provided a model of mannish virtue at a time when Maggy knew no men and now Maggy, who had lost and left a man in America, found herself eager for support. Dizzy could still act with vigour. Look at the way she had rescued Rosheen.

The two – Maggy had heard the story from each separately – had not met for years when one night, a little over a year ago, they sat opposite each other on the North London underground. Rosheen's eyes were red; she had just run out of the house after being kicked in the stomach by Sean. For want of anywhere to go, she was heading for a late-night cinema.

'Leave him,' said Dizzy, 'you can stay in my flat.'

'I love him,' Rosheen told her. 'He needs me. He can't cope by himself. Poor Sean! He's gentle most of the time and when he's not, it's not his fault. He's sick, you see. His mother warned me: Mairéad. It's his nerves. Ulcers. Anyway we're married.'

'All the more reason', Dizzy told her, 'to get out while you can. Are you going to have kids with a

chap like that? You should call the police,' she lec-
tured.

'I couldn't.' Rosheen was an underdog to the
marrow.

'I could.' Dizzy had Anglo-Irish assurance. 'Just
let him come looking for you.' She herded Rosheen
home to her flat and the husband, when he presented himself, was duly given the bum's rush. He took
to ambushing Rosheen, who went back to him twice
but had to slink back to Dizzy after some days with
black eyes and other more secret ailments.

'You're like a cat that goes out on the tiles,' Dizzy
told her. 'You need an interest. You should come to
political rallies with me.'

When Maggy arrived in London and agreed to
move in with the two, Rosheen was working as an
usherette in a theatre where Dizzy was stage man-
ager. The plays put on by the group were revolutionary and much of Dizzy's conversation echoed
their scripts.

'You have a slave mind,' she said without malice
to Maggy, who claimed she was too busy finishing

a thesis to have time for politics. Dizzy did not ask the subject of the thesis – it was semiology – nor show any interest in the years Maggy had spent in America. Having gathered that there had been some sort of man trouble, she preferred to know no more. To Rosheen, who showed more curiosity, Maggy remarked that her situation was much like Rosheen's own.

'Convalescing?'

'Yes.'

'This is a good place to do it,' said Rosheen. 'Though I sometimes think I won't be able to stand it. Sean keeps ringing me up. Crying. And I'm in dread that I'll break down and go back to him. I miss him at night something awful.'

'So why . . .'

'Ah sure it'd never be any good.'

'Is that what Dizzy tells you?'

'Yes. But sure I know myself that when a relationship has gone bad there's no mending it.'

'Relationship' would be Dizzy's word. But Maggy wasn't going to interfere. Rosheen she remembered from their childhood as unmodulated and unskinned: an emotional bomb liable to go off unpredictably. Better let Dizzy handle her. She herself was trying to finish her thesis before her money ran out. She spent her days at the British Museum, coming home as late as 9 p.m. Often a gust of talk would roar into the hallway as she pushed open the door. 'Bourgeois crapology,' she'd hear, or: 'It's bloody *not* within the competence of the minister. Listen, I know the 1937 constitution by heart. D'ya want to bet?' The voices would be Irish, fierce and drunk. Maggy would slip into the kitchen, get herself food as noiselessly as she could manage and withdraw into her room. Towards the evening's end, Rosheen's voice invariably reached her, singing some wailing song and Maggy would have wagered any money that the grief throbbing through it had not a thing to do with politics.

Sometimes, the phone in the hall would ring and Rosheen would have it off the hook before the third peal. It was outside Maggy's bedroom door and she could hear Rosheen whisper to it, her furtive voice muffled by the coats which hung next to it and under which she seemed to plunge her head to hide perhaps from Dizzy.

'You're drunk,' she'd start. 'You are. Sean, you're not to ring here, I told you. I suppose they've just shut the pub . . . it's not that, no . . . even if you were cold stone sober I'd say the same . . . Listen, why don't you go to bed and sleep it off? Have you eaten anything? What about your ulcer? Listen, go and get a glass of milk somewhere . . . you can . . . I can't . . . it's not that. I do. I do know my own mind but . . . She's not a dyke, Sean . . . You know as well as I do it'd never work . . . If only you'd take the cure . . . Well it's a vicious circle then, isn't it? . . . Please, Sean, ah don't be that way, Sean . . . I do but . . . ah Sean . . .'

Sooner or later there would be the click of the phone. Rosheen would stand for a while among the coats, then open the door to go into the front room. Later, she would be singing again, this time something subdued like one of the hymns which they had sung together in school. This tended to put a damper on the party and the guests would clatter out shortly afterwards.

Next day smells of stale beer and ash pervaded the flat, and Rosheen's voice, raised in the shower, pierced through the slap of water to reach a half-sleeping Maggy.

Mo-o-other of Christ,
Sta-a-ar of the sea,
Pra-a-ay for the wanderer,
Pray for me.

'You missed a good evening,' Dizzy reproached. 'I don't know why you can't be sociable. Mix. There were interesting, committed people there. One was a fellow who escaped from Long Kesh.'

'I have reading to do.'

'Piffle! Do you good to get away from your books. Live. Open yourself to new experiences.'

The man Maggy had lived with in San Francisco had made similar reproaches. Books, he said, made Maggy egocentric. Squirrelling away ideas, she was trying to cream the world's mind. His was a sentient generation, he told her, but she reminded him of the joke about the guy caught committing necrophilia whose defence was that he'd taken the corpse to be a live Englishwoman.

'Irish.'

Irish, English – what was the difference? It was her coldness which had challenged him. He was a man who relished difficulty. Beneath her cold crust he'd counted on finding lava and instead what he'd found inside was colder still: like eating baked Alaska. Maggy, feeling that she was in violation of some emotional equivalent of the Trade Descriptions Act, blamed everything on her First Communion. She'd been rejected by her maker, she explained, thrown on the reject heap and inhibited since. This mollified her lover and they took an affectionate leave of each other. Now, in wintry London, where men like him were as rare as humming birds, she groaned with afterclaps of lust.

Well, if her thaw was untimely, the fault was her own.

What was really too bad was that Rosheen, who had passed the First Communion test with flying colours, should be unable to consummate her punctual passions. She was slurping out feeling now, steaming and singing in the shower while the other two ate breakfast.

Mother of Chri-i-ist . . .

'How was your First Communion?' Maggy asked Dizzy. 'Did you experience ecstasy?'

'I don't think anyone mentioned the word. I thought of it more as a way of joining the club. As a convert, you know.'

'*Sta-a-a-r of the . . .* Fuck!' Rosheen had dropped the shampoo. Now they would all get glass splinters in their feet.

'Didn't you notice the prayers?' Maggy wondered. *'May thy wounds be to me food and drink by which I may be nourished, inebriated and overjoyed!* Surely you remember that? And: *Thou alone will ever be my hope, my riches, my delight, my pleasure, my joy . . . My fragrance, my sweet savour?* It goes on.'

'Do you think bloody Rosheen's cut herself? It's

a responsibility having her around. I didn't think you were pious, Maggy. More toast?'

'I saw it all', said Maggy, 'as a promise of what I'd find outside the convent: men like Christs who'd provide all that.'

'I do think semiology is the wrong thing for you, Maggy. You should put your energies into something practical.'

'Dizzy, you're a treat! You've been trying to de-Anglicize yourself since the day we met, but your officer-class genes are too much for you.'

This was going too far. Dizzy, hurt, had to be sweetened by a gift of liqueur jam for which Maggy had to go all the way to Harrods. The trip made her late and when she got back to the flat Dizzy had left for the local pub. Maggy, joining her there, found her chatting to a man who sometimes dropped in after work. He was a sandy-haired chap who probably worked in an insurance office. Dizzy imagined him as starved for life and in search of anecdotes. 'I drop into an Irish pub in Camden,' he would tell his wife who would be wearing an apron covered with Campari ads. Dizzy, nourishing this imagined saga, had tried to get Rosheen to sing while he was in the pub, though it was always too early and the ambience wasn't right. 'It *is* an IRA pub, you know,' she had told him, slipping in and out of Irishness as though it were stage make-up.

'I believe less and less in democracy,' she was saying when Maggy arrived. 'Hullo, Maggy. What're you having? Don't you agree that democracy is a con? Do you know who said "the people have no right to do wrong"? Also "there are rights which a minority may justly uphold in arms against a majority"? Bet you don't.'

The man in the belted mac and sandy hair had nothing to say to this. Dizzy, however, could carry on two ends of a conversation.

'You might say,' she supplied, 'that the people have a right to decide for themselves. But "the people" are people like that gutless wonder, Sean. *They* never initiate change, so . . .'

Maggy left for the loo. Through its window she saw Sean and Rosheen embracing in the damp and empty garden of the pub. Both seemed to be crying.

It might, however, be rain on their cheeks. She went back to the lounge.

'Saw it in Malaya,' the macintoshed man was saying. 'Bulk of the people were loyal. Just a few agitators. You've got to string 'em up right at the start. Cut off the gangrened limb. Else you'll have chaos.'

'But I', said Dizzy, 'was speaking *on behalf* of the agitators, the leaven, the heroes!'

'Oh,' the man moved his glass away from hers. 'I could hardly go along with that.'

Rosheen stood at the door of the lounge and beckoned Maggy behind Dizzy's back. She put a finger on her lips.

'I'm going.' Maggy got up.

Rosheen rushed Maggy down a corridor. 'Let's get out of here. That man's in the Special Branch. A detective. He's looking for Sean.'

'Why . . . but then Dizzy . . .?'

'Dizzy's an eejit, doesn't know whether she's coming or going.'

'You think Dizzy's an eejit?' Maggy couldn't have
been more astonished if a worm had stood erect on
its tail and spoken.

'You know she is, Maggy! She's in way over her
head. Wait till I tell you.' Rosheen's eyes were red,
but she spoke lucidly. 'It's Sean they're after. They
want him to turn informer and if he doesn't, they'll
spread the word that he *has*. Then the IRA will get
him. And you know what *they* do to informers.'

'Are you sure?' Maggy asked, but it was likely
enough. She remembered Mairéad's description of
the nerve-shot Sean. He was the very stuff of which
the police could hope to make an informer. His
family had a record. Had he one himself? 'Is he
political?' she asked.

'No, but they could nail him. They can nail anyone.'

'But what does he *know*? I mean what information has he?'

'That's the trouble,' Rosheen told her. 'He doesn't
know much at all. But in self-defence he'll have to
shop someone and the only one he can think of is
Dizzy.'

'Dizzy?'

'You see she's not real IRA: only on the fringe, expendable. Sean thinks they mightn't mind about her. The IRA, I mean. And naturally *he* hates her.' Rosheen blushed and added quickly, 'This is killing him. He's passing blood again. Both sides have their eye on him now. He's been seen talking to that detective, so if anything at all happens in the next few weeks, it'll be blemt on Sean. I think he's a dead man.' Rosheen spoke numbly. 'If one lot doesn't get him, the others will.'

'And what *is* Dizzy up to? I mean what could he tell them?'

Rosheen turned stunned eyes on Maggy, who saw that there was no turning *her* into an Emerald Pimpernel. Dizzy, having stumbled onto territory which Rosheen knew better, might be revealed as an eejit and a play-actress but Rosheen herself, helpless as a heifer who has somehow strayed onto the centre divider of a highway, could only wait and wonder whether the traffic of events might be miraculously diverted before it mowed her down.

'What do they get expendable people like her to do?' she asked. 'Plant bombs.'

Dizzy, when faced with the question, reacted violently: 'Maggy, are you working for the Special Branch? Shit, I should have known! All that pretence at being apathetic – or', her eyes narrowed, 'is it Rosheen who's been talking? I always thought Sean had the stuff of a stool pigeon.' She went on like this until Maggy cut her short with the news that who *was* in the Special Branch was Dizzy's drinking companion whose phone number Maggy – thanks to Rosheen – was in a position to let her have.

'It's a Scotland Yard number. Check if you like,' she said, astounded at the way Dizzy's authority had crumbled. It was like the emperor's clothes: an illusion, nothing but RADA vowels, that officer-class demeanour, thought Maggy, who now felt powerful and practical herself. Rosheen, like one of those creatures in folk tales who hand the heroine some magic tool, had made Maggy potent.

In return, the helper must herself be helped. Maggy remembered Rosheen's telephone colloquies with Sean seeping, regularly as bedtime stories, under her own bedroom door and that Rosheen's renunciatory voice had quavered like a captive bird's as she hid among the heavy coats in Dizzy's front hall. Now she must be allowed to unleash her precarious passion in peace.

'*You're* a security risk, you must see that,' said Maggy to Dizzy, making short work of her protests. 'So you'd better let me pick up your bomb. Never mind why I want to. That's my concern. Motives', she told her, 'are irrelevant to history. If I do this for the IRA, I shall be IRA. Wasn't that your own calculation?'

This bit of rhetoric proved truer than foreseen, for a number of squat, tough-faced, under-nourished-looking people turned up at her trial and had to be cleared from the public gallery where they created a disturbance and gave clenched-fist salutes. They seemed to have co-opted her act, and her lawyer brought along copies of excitable weekly papers which described it in terms she could not follow because their references were rancorous and obscure. One was called *An Phoblacht,* another *The Starry Plough* and there was a sad daily from Belfast full of ads for money-lenders, in memoriam columns and, for her, a bleak fraternity. Dizzy did not come and neither did Rosheen.

Who did attend the trial and visit her afterwards was the glass-eyed man. 'All Ireland is with you,' he said, 'all true Irish Socialist Republicans.' Was this a joke? Did the eye gleam with irony? Or had he meant that her act was public property, whether she liked this or not, and despite the fact that her victim had not been Dizzy's target at all? *That* was to have been a building and there was to have been a telephone warning to avoid loss of life. Maggy thought this ridiculous. A war was a war and everyone knew how those warnings went wrong. The police delayed acting so as to rouse public feeling against the bombers – for how much anger could be generated if explosions hurt nobody, going off with the mild bang of a firework display? Property owners would be indignant, but the police needed wider support than theirs. Yes, the police were undoubtedly the culprits. They bent rules. Detective Inspector Coffee had been bending rules when he told the nerve-shot Sean that he'd put the word about in Irish pubs that Sean was an informer unless he became one. An old police trick! It had landed men in a ditch with a bullet in the neck before now. How many had Detective Inspector Coffee nudged that way? How many more would he? None, because Maggy had got him with Dizzy's bomb.

'For personal reasons,' she told Glass Eye.

'It's *what* you did that counts.'

What she had done astounded her. She had been like one of those mothers who find the sudden strength to lift lorries and liberate their child. Unthinkingly, almost in a trance, she had phoned the number given her by Rosheen and asked for an appointment. She had information of interest, she promised, and evidence to back it up. Could she bring it round at once? Where she'd got the number? Oh, please, she didn't want to say this on the phone. *'They* may be listening, watching. Maybe I'm paranoid but I've got caught up in something terrifying. By chance.'

Her genuinely shaky voice convinced him and he proved more guileless than she could have believed for she had gone to the meeting fearful of being frisked by attendant heavies. But no. There were no preliminaries. She got straight to the man himself.

'Detective Inspector Coffee?'

He was the sandy-haired chap all right. Perhaps he had recognized her voice on the phone? She handed him a bag. There were documents on top of the device which was primed to go off when touched.

'I brought you papers. You'll see what they are. I'm afraid I'm a bit rattled. Nausea. Could I find a loo?'

He showed her the way, then walked back into his room. She was two flights down the stairs, when she heard the explosion. Oddly – she had expected her fake nausea to become real – she felt nothing but elation. There were shattering noises, shouts, a

bell. She thought: that's put an end to his smile, his
assurance, his smug, salary-drawing, legal murder.
The word registered then and, seeing him in her
mind's eye blown apart, she began to sweat. The
smell was pungent when she reached the outer door
where a policeman stopped her.

'You'll demand political status?' asked the glass-
eyed man. 'Go on hunger strike until they grant it.'

'Political?'

He was impatient, the visit nearly over. A group
in another wing of the prison were all set to strike.
He was planning publicity which would have more
impact if she joined in. 'Listen, love,' he said,
'you're political or what are you?'

Political? The notion exhilarated. Old songs. Solidarity. We shall overcome. In gaol, as in church,
that sort of language seemed to work. On a snap
decision, she agreed and, in after-image, the gleam
of his eye pinned her to the definition. As she grew
weaker, her weathercock mind froze at North-
North-East. The strike gave purpose to her days
and, like the falling sparrow's, her pain became a

47

usable statistic. 'Get involved,' commanded an ad in the *Irish News* which the glass-eyed man brought on a subsequent visit. '*They* did.' A list of hunger-strikers included Maggy's name.

Her mind was flickering. Sharp-edged scenes faltered and she wondered whether thin people like herself had less stamina than others. It was too soon, surely, to be so weak? She had a fantasy – some of the time it was a conviction – that her lover from San Francisco had come and that they had done together all the things she – no: he – had always wanted to do. Like a drowning person's flash vision of a lifetime, a whole erotic frieze unrolled with convincing brilliance in her mind. Sensory deprivation was supposed to make you hallucinate, she remembered, but confused this false prison visitor with real ones. His eyes gleamed like glass. 'Sentient,' he had said of himself and 'cold' of her, but her memory of him was bright like ice and cold. She *was* cold. It was part of her condition. And her mouth was dry. In her fantasy – or reality? – he offered her an icicle to suck.

'Don't talk,' said someone, 'save your saliva.'

Now her lover was lying naked and wounded beside her and offered her his wounds to moisten her lips, but they too were dry and not as food and drink to her at all.

Vitamins and hormones were being used up.

This was the prison doctor talking now. He had checked her blood and urine and felt it his duty to warn her that irreversible effects could occur.

'Jaundice,' warned the doctor.

'Golden, gilded skin,' said her lover. 'Here,' he presented her with a golden potato chip. 'Eat this for me.'

'Eat,' said the screw.

'Do yourself a favour,' said the doctor.

Maggy put the chip in her mouth. It was dry. She couldn't swallow it. It revived her nausea.